P9-DVQ-283

GIANT PEACH Yodel

GIANT PEACH *yodel*

By Jan Peck   Illustrated by Barry Root

PELICAN PUBLISHING COMPANY

GRETNA 2012

Library of Congress Cataloging-in-Publication Data

Peck, Jan.
  Giant peach yodel / by Jan Peck ; illustrated by Barry Root.
    p. cm.
  Summary: In a retelling of a Russian folktale set in the American
south, little Buddy Earl keeps his family from being the laughingstock
of the county Peach Pickin' Festival. Includes a recipe for peach cobbler.
  ISBN 978-1-58980-980-2 (hardcover : alk. paper) [1. Folklore—Russia.]
I. Root, Barry, ill. II. Turnip. English. III. Title.

  PZ8.1.P33Gj 2011
  398.2—dc22
  [E]

                  2011002911

Printed in Singapore
Published by Pelican Publishing Company, Inc.
1000 Burmaster Street, Gretna, Louisiana 70053

Giant Peach Yodel

One summer day, Tall Papa Tom hopped into his old jalopy and hollered, "I'm fixin' to head out to the Peach-Pickin' Festival!" He honked the horn. *AAAAOOOOGAAAA!*

Pretty Mama May sauntered out and plopped into the truck next to Tall Papa Tom. Sweet Sister Isabelle skipped out and leapt into the seat beside Pretty Mama May.

Then the screen door flew open and out raced Little Buddy Earl. He sprang into the seat behind Sweet Sister Isabelle.

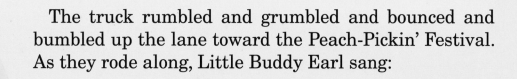

The truck rumbled and grumbled and bounced and bumbled up the lane toward the Peach-Pickin' Festival. As they rode along, Little Buddy Earl sang:

"Corn in the fields,
How do you do?
I love grits
And yodel-ay-dee-hoo!"

"Well, for fleas in a frying pan," said Sweet Sister Isabelle. "Little Buddy Earl sure can yodel. But what's the use of that?"

The truck rumbled and grumbled and bounced and bumbled up the gravel road toward the Peach-Pickin' Festival. As they rode along, Little Buddy Earl sang:

"Tomatoes in the fields,
How do you do?
I love ketchup
And yodel-ay-dee-hoo!"

"Well, that's the all-overest thing I ever heard,"
said Pretty Mama May. "Little Buddy Earl sure
can yodel. But what's the use of that?"

The truck rumbled and grumbled and bounced and bumbled up the lane toward the Peach-Pickin' Festival. As they rode along, Little Buddy Earl sang:

"Dewberries on the bushes,
How do you do?
I love jelly
And yodel-ay-dee-hoo!"

Tall Papa Tom scratched his head.
"Well, stomp my boot! Little Buddy
Earl sure can yodel. But what's the
use of that?"

When they got up yonder, Tall Papa Tom honked the horn. *AAAAOOOOGAAAA!*

Out ran Cousin Thumb-Sucker Tucker, Long Lanky Spanky, and Lean Annie Jean. Aunt Evelina Josephina and Cranky Uncle Frankie followed right behind them.

They hugged and kissed and everyone talked all at once. Then Cranky Uncle Frankie showed them the peach orchard.

"These are some sorry-lookin' peaches,"
he said. "We're gonna be the laughin'stock
of the whole county!"

Little Buddy Earl looked up and sang to a peach:

"One little peach,
How do you do?
I love cobbler
And yodel-ay-dee-hoo!"

And as he sang, that peach grew and grew and grew.

The peach was as tall as Papa Tom, as pretty as Mama May, and as red as Aunt Evelina Josephina's hair.

The grownups yelled, "You young'uns get outta the way! Let us big folks pick this peach." Tall Papa Tom, Pretty Mama May, Aunt Evelina Josephina, and Cranky Uncle Frankie stood on their toes as high as they could. They stretched and they craned and they reached and they strained. *"Grrrrhhhh!"* But that giant peach just wouldn't let loose.

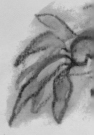

"OK, you young'uns!" the grownups finally called. "Hitch up your sleeves and help us pick this peach."

The kids yelled, "Sure thang!"

So Long Lanky Spanky and Lean Annie Jean climbed on top of the grownups' shoulders. Sweet Sister Isabelle and Cousin Thumb-Sucker Tucker climbed on top of the big kids' shoulders. And they stretched and they craned and they reached and they strained. *"Grrrrhhhh!"* But that giant peach just wouldn't let loose.

Little Buddy Earl yelled, "I can pick that peach!"

All his cousins, his aunt and uncle, his sister, and his mother and father laughed.

Cranky Uncle Frankie said, "Well, don't just stand there—shake a leg! Let's see what you can do."

So the big kids climbed back on top of the grownups' shoulders, and the little kids climbed back on top of the big kids' shoulders, and Little Buddy Earl stood at the very, very tiptop and sang:

"Yodel-ay-dee-hoo,
I'll sing a bit.
I love my peach
To the pit!
One giant peach,
Growin' in the tree,
I'll pick you
And yodel-ay-dee-hee!"

The peach began to twist and twirl and swing and whirl, and when Little Buddy Earl yodeled a high note—*"yodel-ay-dee-hoooo!"*—that giant peach popped right off the stem.

"*Look out!*" yelled Cranky Uncle Frankie.

That peach rumbled and grumbled and bounced and bumbled and plopped right into the back of Tall Papa Tom's old jalopy.

Cranky Uncle Frankie smiled. "Well, for pockets on a pig. Little Buddy Earl sure can yodel! Now we'll be the talk of the peach festival. That yodelin' is sure good for something!"

And later that day, the old jalopy cruised right down Main Street in the Peach-Pickin' Festival Parade. That giant peach shone mighty fine.

Tall Papa Tom honked the horn. *AAAAOOOOGAAAA!*
And Little Buddy Earl sat on top as the Peach-Pickin',
Yodel-Singin', Ever-Lovin' King.

"Yodel-ay-dee-hoooo!"

Little Buddy Earl's Peach Cobbler
(Ask your family to help you.)

1½ cups flour
1 cup sugar
Pinch of salt
1½ sticks butter (softened)
Cold water

Preheat oven to 350 degrees.
Mix flour, sugar, and salt together really well.
Cut butter into flour mixture until crumbly.
Add enough cold water for a thick dough.
Roll dough out on a floured board until about ¼ inch thick.

2 cans (1 lb. 13 oz. each) peaches
1 cup sugar
2 tsp. cinnamon

Mix together peaches, sugar, and cinnamon.
Pour fruit mixture into a well-greased rectangular baking pan and top with strips of the dough in a crisscross pattern.
Sprinkle additional sugar and cinnamon over the top.
Bake for about 40-50 minutes or until golden brown.
You can serve it right out of the pan, warm, or at room temperature. Top with ice cream. Yodel yummy!

Note: This is an old, old recipe, which I got from a 100-year-old German lady who cooked delicious lunches for our school cafeteria. We all loved that peach cobbler at our little country school in Azle, Texas.